The Field Museum of Natural History

MUSEUMS OF THE WORLD

By Joy Gregory

MEDIA ENHANCED BOOKS

AV2 BY WEIGL™

ADDED VALUE • AUDIO VISUAL

www.av2books.com

AV² provides enriched content that supplements and complements this book. Weigl's AV² books strive to create inspired learning and engage young minds in a total learning experience.

Your AV² Media Enhanced books come alive with...

Audio
Listen to sections of the book read aloud.

Key Words
Study vocabulary, and complete a matching word activity.

Video
Watch informative video clips.

Quizzes
Test your knowledge.

Embedded Weblinks
Gain additional information for research.

Slide Show
View images and captions, and prepare a presentation.

Try This!
Complete activities and hands-on experiments.

... and much, much more!

Go to **www.av2books.com**, and enter this book's unique code.

BOOK CODE

M 2 8 5 8 6 9

AV² by Weigl brings you media enhanced books that support active learning.

Published by AV² by Weigl
350 5th Avenue, 59th Floor
New York, NY 10118

Websites: www.av2books.com www.weigl.com

Library of Congress Cataloging-in-Publication Data
Gregory, Joy (Joy Marie), author.
 The Field Museum of Natural History / Joy Gregory.
    pages cm. -- (Museums of the world)
ISBN 978-1-4896-3252-4 (hardcover : alk. paper) -- ISBN 978-1-4896-3253-1 (softcover : alk. paper) --
ISBN 978-1-4896-3254-8 (single-user ebk.) -- ISBN 978-1-4896-3255-5 (multi-user ebk.)
1. Field Museum of Natural History--Juvenile literature. 2. Natural history museums--Illinois--Chicago--
Juvenile literature. 3. Chicago (Ill.)--Buildings, structures, etc.--Juvenile literature. I. Title.

 QH70.U62C54 2016
 508.074'773'11--dc23
                    2014038746

Printed in Brainerd, Minnesota, in the United States of America
1 2 3 4 5 6 7 8 9 0 18 17 16 15 14

122014
WEP051214

Editor: Heather Kissock
Design: Dean Pickup

Every reasonable effort has been made to trace ownership and to obtain permission to reprint copyright material. The publishers would be pleased to have any errors or omissions brought to their attention so that they may be corrected in subsequent printings.

Weigl acknowledges Getty Images, Alamy, Newscom, Corbis, iStock, and Dreamstime as its primary image suppliers for this title.

Contents

What Is the Field Museum?

Located in Chicago, Illinois, the Field Museum holds one of the world's most extensive natural history **collections**. Natural history museums tell the story of planet Earth and the people, animals, and plants that have lived on it—now or in the past. Officially called the Field Museum of Natural History, the Field Museum helps visitors understand how the natural world has developed and changed over time.

The Field Museum is the centerpiece of Chicago's Museum Campus, which also includes the Adler Planetarium and Shedd Aquarium.

Natural history museums store and display specimens and artifacts that teach visitors about the natural world. Specimens are examples of items that occur naturally, such as **fossils**, plants, and rocks. Artifacts are items made by people. The Field Museum holds fossils from every major dinosaur group. The *Inside Ancient Egypt* **exhibit** includes actual mummies and a **shrine** to a cat goddess. Other exhibits teach visitors about people from around the world, including Africa, Asia, and the South Pacific.

The Field Museum covers
more than
480,000 square feet
(44,594 square meters)
of exhibit space.

The museum has more than
26 million
specimens and artifacts in its collections.

Approximately
1.25 million people
visit the museum every year.

About 140 scientists
work for the Field Museum.

History of the Field Museum

In 1893, Chicago hosted the World's Columbian Exposition, or World's Fair. As part of the planning process, the organizers wanted the fair to have a lasting effect on the city. They decided that they would create a museum from the fair's exhibits. Local businesspeople donated money to the museum so that it could purchase the items exhibited by countries attending the World's Fair. The largest of these donations came from a man named Marshall Field, who gave the organizers $1 million. When the museum opened, it was called the Field Columbian Museum in his honor.

Chicago's World's Fair featured displays from 46 countries, as well as many of the U.S. states.

1894 The Field Columbian Museum opens in Chicago's Jackson Park.

1914 Construction of a new Field Museum building begins in Grant Park.

1875 — 1900 — 1910 — 1925

1905 The museum changes its name to the Field Museum of Natural History to emphasize the content of its collections.

1921 The new Field Museum building opens on the site where it still stands today.

1922–1924 The museum expands its exhibitions through several **expeditions**.

The Field Columbian Museum was located on the grounds of the World's Fair, in the Palace of Fine Arts building.

1945 The Field Museum begins to focus more on scientific research and less on adding new specimens and artifacts to its collections.

2005 The museum opens the Collections Resource Center to create more storage space for its specimens and artifacts.

1950   1975   2000   2010

1962 The museum hosts the Egyptian exhibition, *Tutankhamun Treasures*.

2006 *Evolving Planet*, a new **permanent exhibit**, is launched. The exhibit gives people a look at 4 billion years of life on Earth.

2009 The museum opens its 3D, or **three-dimensional**, theater, the first of its kind in Chicago.

The Founders

Establishing the Field Museum was a group effort, requiring the resources of many people. The people working on the World's Fair organizing committee supplied the vision for the project. However, the project needed funding to become a reality. It was not until Marshall Field made his large donation that the museum really began to take form.

Marshall Field (1834–1906)

Marshall Field was born on a farm in Massachusetts and, by age 16, was working in a local store. He moved to Chicago when he was 21 and quickly rose through the ranks of a **mercantile house** to become a full partner. Field left his job at the mercantile house in 1865 to work at a dry goods store. Over time, he bought the store and developed it into a full-fledged department store. By the 1890s, Marshall Field & Company was the dominant department store in Chicago. The success of the company allowed Field to invest in real estate and other industries. When he died in 1906, his estate was worth $125 million.

Marshall Field left an additional $8 million to the museum in his will.

Edward E. Ayer (1841–1927)

Edward E. Ayer was born in Kenosha, Wisconsin and later lived in Illinois. At age 19, he moved to Nevada and then California to find work. Following the Civil War, he returned to Illinois, where he made his fortune selling timber for railroad construction. Ayer was one of the first people to support the creation of a museum in Chicago. He sat on the museum association's finance committee and became the museum's first president. He also talked Marshall Field into making his first donation.

Edward E. Ayer was an avid collector of American Indian artifacts. His collection was eventually donated to the Field Museum.

Frederic Ward Putnam (1839–1915)

Born in Salem, Massachusetts, Frederic Ward Putnam showed an early interest in nature. In 1856, he went to Harvard College and became an assistant to a prominent **naturalist**. Putnam left Harvard without graduating, but was able to secure **curatorial** positions in several museums before returning to Harvard to teach **ethnology**. In 1891, he began organizing an exhibit for the Chicago World's Fair. The contents of this exhibit became the foundation of the Field Museum's collection.

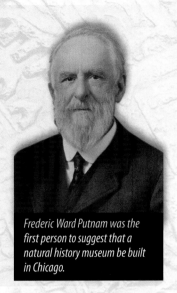

Frederic Ward Putnam was the first person to suggest that a natural history museum be built in Chicago.

Frederick J. V. Skiff (1851–1921)

Frederick J. V. Skiff was one of the organizers of the Chicago World's Fair, supervising the fair's mining and metals exhibits. When the idea of establishing a museum began to take shape, he made arrangements with his exhibitors to secure display pieces for the museum. Skiff's skill as a supervisor impressed the museum's planners. They asked him to become the director of the new museum. He accepted and remained in this position until his death in 1921.

Frederick J. V. Skiff also helped organize exhibits at the Paris World's Fair in 1900 and the St. Louis World's Fair in 1906.

Harlow Higinbotham (1838–1919)

Harlow Higinbotham served as president of the World's Columbian Exposition. A partner at Marshall Field & Company, Higinbotham brought a wealth of experience to the job and played a key role in the fair's success. He was in full support of creating a museum and served as the chairman of the museum's executive committee. After Edward E. Ayer retired, Higinbotham became the museum's president.

Harlow Higinbotham bought several collections for the Field Museum, including its gem and mineral collection.

The Field Museum Today

The Field Museum's exhibits have captivated visitors for more than 100 years. Over time, the Field Museum has evolved, adding new features to its exhibits that help bring natural history to life for visitors. Many of the exhibits now provide visitors with the opportunity to experience natural history in new ways. For example, people can watch 3D movies about the world's smallest and largest species. They can also walk into a **replica** of an ancient Egyptian tomb. The Field Museum has become known throughout the world for its creative approach to education.

The museum's entrance hall provides a sneak peak at a sample of the treasures displayed in the museum.

Ground Level

The ground level features the museum's *Inside Ancient Egypt* and *Underground Adventure* exhibits. It is also home to the museum's education department, which is made up of classrooms and meeting rooms as well as a library and a theater.

Main Level

Visitors to the museum's main level can learn more about the world's peoples and animals. The main hall is home to Sue, the world's largest and most complete fossil of a Tyrannosaurus Rex.

Upper Level

The upper level houses the museum's main dinosaur exhibit and its *Evolving Planet* exhibit. The museum's plant and gem collections are also on this floor, along with its exhibits on peoples of the Pacific.

Touring the Field Museum

The Field Museum offers visitors a variety of things to see and do. Besides its galleries of specimens and artifacts, there are also laboratories. Here, people can watch scientists at work and participate in some of the activities taking place.

Halls of the Ancient Americas These galleries take visitors on a trip back in time to show what life was like for Ancient Americans living on these continents. Visitors can find out what it was like to hunt mammoths in the Ice Age as well as walk through an ancient Aztec city. The galleries focus on the changes that have occurred over the course of history and their impact on today's society.

On display in the Field Museum's Hall of the Ancient Americas is a copy of an Aztec Sun Stone that was found in 1790.

Bengal tigers are just one of the animals featured in the dioramas in the Hall of Asian Mammals.

Hall of Asian Mammals
Visitors to this gallery are given the opportunity to learn more about the animals of Asia. The gallery uses **dioramas** to show how the animals live in their natural **habitats**. The collections include specimens of giant pandas, leopards, and a variety of birds.

McDonald's Fossil Preparation Laboratory

The McDonald's Fossil Prep Lab is one of three fossil labs at the museum. It is here that the museum's scientists examine fossils and prepare them for display. The lab has glass windows, allowing visitors to watch the scientists as they work.

Visitors to the lab can see the various types of equipment scientists use to remove fossils from the stones in which they were found.

DNA Discovery Center

The DNA Discovery Center features displays that explore the role that **deoxyribonucleic acid (DNA)** plays in **biodiversity**. At the center's DNA lab, scientists analyze DNA from thousands of species. Visitors can watch and ask questions as scientists do their work.

Displays in the DNA Discovery Center help explain how different organisms can share similar genetic codes.

It cost **$7 million** to build the current Field Museum in 1914.

$ $ $ $ $ $ $

Tables in the Fossil Prep Lab are strong enough to hold **2,000-pound** (907-kilogram) **rocks**.

The Hall of Ancient Americas contains more than **2,200 artifacts**.

Only **1%** of the Field Museum's artifacts are **on display** at any given time.

The museum's library has more than **250,000 volumes** in its collection.

The Field Museum is **open every day except Christmas.**

The *Evolving Planet's* "Magdalenian Woman" skeleton is at least **12,000 years old**.

The museum bought Sue the T-Rex in 1997 for **$8.36 million**.

The Maori meeting house is covered with hundreds of face carvings. **No two faces are the same.**

The Hall of Gems has an Egyptian necklace that is **more than 3,400 years old.**

 The museum's Aztec Sun Stone **measures** 12 feet (3.7 m) across and weighs 24.3 tons (22 tonnes).

The museum's bird division holds more than **70,000 bird skeletons.**

Treasures of the Field Museum

As a natural history museum, the Field Museum shows the history of the world through plants, animals, and people. In doing this, the museum encourages visitors to learn about the natural world and how it has evolved over time. It also asks them to consider whether the changes that have taken place have been beneficial to the planet. Some of the plant and animal specimens found at the museum are of species no longer living on Earth. Displaying their remains in the museum draws attention to the issue of **conservation**.

The Field Museum arranges its exhibits by theme. American Indian masks are found in the Northwest Coast and Arctic Peoples exhibit.

Sue This Tyrannosaurus Rex fossil is one of the Field Museum's star attractions. It is named after the fossil hunter who found the remains in 1990. With 58 dagger-like teeth, Sue stands 13 feet (4 m) tall from floor to hip and 42 feet (13 m) long from snout to tail.

The skeleton on exhibit features a copy of Sue's skull. The original skull is kept in a display case on the museum's upper level balcony.

Lions of Tsavo In 1898, two lions terrorized the people who lived and worked near the Tsavo River in East Africa. The lions reportedly killed 135 people before they were shot by a railroad engineer. The Field Museum bought their skulls and skins in 1924 for $5,000. They are now displayed on the museum's main level.

After performing a series of tests on the bones and hair of the lions, scientists now believe that the two males were responsible for only about 35 deaths.

Shrine to Bastet The *Inside Ancient Egypt* gallery is home to the Shrine to Bastet, the cat goddess. The ancient Egyptians worshipped cats because they protected crops and homes from snakes and rodents. The exhibit includes a bronze sculpture of Bastet, which is believed to hold a mummified cat.

A statue of Sekhmet, the Egyptian goddess of war, stands in front of the Shrine to Bastet. While Bastet is portrayed as a kind cat, Sekhmet is the more aggressive lion.

Pawnee Earth Lodge This full-sized replica of a Pawnee home lets visitors step back into the 1800s, when earth lodges were found on the plains of Nebraska. Visitors can walk inside the lodge to see the clothing, cooking tools, weapons, and toys used by Pawnee people in the past.

Members of the Pawnee Nation advised the Field Museum on the lodge's design and its contents.

Collection Conservation

The Field Museum contains artifacts and specimens that are thousands of years old. They need special care to ensure that they do not break or become damaged. The Field Museum has a team of conservators that work to maintain its collection of natural history artifacts. These specialists use a variety of techniques to assess the condition of each piece and learn what it is made from. They then take steps to protect it and prevent it from deteriorating.

Light on the Subject

Shining light on an artifact or specimen allows conservators to study the surface of the object. The light is shone on the object at different angles to allow for a thorough examination. The conservators take note of any problem areas, such as signs of deterioration or previous repairs. They then plan a care program for the pieces.

Besides using light to inspect artifacts, conservators also rely on it when working on repairs and restoration.

Imaging Some artifacts require an internal assessment. X-rays let conservators look at what is below the surface of an artifact or specimen. This allows them to see how an artifact was made and whether there are any weaknesses inside. Some artifacts contain other artifacts. A mummy case, for instance, usually holds a mummy. X-rays help conservators determine the condition of the interior artifacts.

X-rays help conservators examine the contents of mummy cases. They can see if there is a mummy inside and gain insight into its condition.

Climate Control
Artifacts and specimens can be very sensitive to **humidity** levels. Too much moisture in the air can cause mold to grow on some types of materials. Low moisture levels can make items brittle. It is important for conservators to understand how different materials react to moisture. They can then regulate humidity levels in display and storage areas to suit individual pieces.

Maintaining appropriate humidity levels is critical in the Field Museum due to the age and fragile structure of many of its specimens.

Desalinization
Many of the pottery artifacts in the Field Museum's collections were buried underground for thousands of years. Over time, they became contaminated by ground salts. When the humidity changes, the salt **crystallizes**. This causes the surface of the artifact to flake and break apart. To combat this deterioration, conservators often soak the pottery in **deionized** water. The water pulls the salt from the artifact.

Almost one-quarter of the 15,000 ceramic pieces in the museum's Central and South America collections show salt damage.

The Field Museum in the World

The Field Museum works hard to educate people about the natural history of Earth. Museum staff create exhibits and programs to show people how the artifacts and specimens in the museum's collections relate to their lives. Some of these programs are designed for visitors to the museum. Others have been designed to reach out to people all over the world.

Meet a Scientist On Friday mornings, Field Museum scientists come out from behind the scenes to spend time in the museum's galleries. Visitors can listen to them talk about the exhibits and learn about their current research projects. The scientists often bring artifacts and specimens that are not on display in the museum. Visitors are encouraged to ask questions and examine these artifacts up close. Topics vary from week to week and from exhibit to exhibit.

The Meet a Scientist sessions are free with basic admission.

School Programs Schoolchildren of all ages come to the Field Museum for guided tours of particular exhibitions. Others participate in hands-on scientific programs where they make pottery or discover what it is like to hunt for fossils, collect and classify plants, or extract DNA. The museum also allows teachers to borrow artifacts and specimens for use in classroom studies.

The Field Museum's Dozin' with the Dinos program allows school-aged children to have a sleepover in Dinosaur Hall.

I Dig Science The Field Museum is active in the digital world. Its *I Dig Science* program uses technology to connect high school students from U.S. cities with scientists working in the field. Using 3D media, students participate in virtual archaeological digs with the scientists. By communicating directly with the scientists, they see how information is extracted from specimens and artifacts through scientific study. The students then work together to create virtual exhibits based on what they have learned.

Scientists with the Field Museum work on projects all over the world. Some scientists work on the study of animal life. Others go on archaeological digs to learn more about ancient cultures.

Traveling Exhibitions

The Field Museum uses traveling exhibitions to share its collections with the world. Items for these mobile displays are drawn from the museum's permanent exhibitions and sent to museums around the world. Topics range from ancient human civilizations to the conservation of biodiversity. One of the traveling exhibits includes a full-sized replica of Sue.

Besides sending its own exhibits to other museums, the Field Museum also brings in exhibits from other places. In 2006, the Field Museum hosted the Egyptian government's traveling exhibit on the ancient Egyptian pharaoh King Tutankhamun.

Looking to the Future

The Field Museum is committed to learning more about the natural history of Earth and sharing its knowledge with the public. Its scientists continue to gather new artifacts and specimens from all over the world for study. They also continue to study the objects already in their collections to gain deeper insight. In 2014, Field Museum scientists announced that they had discovered at least 126 new species of **fungus**. By comparing their collection to those of other museums, they also discovered three new species of bats.

The three species of yellow-shouldered bats discovered by Field Museum scientists are completely new to science.

The museum works hard to ensure that it is providing new experiences for its visitors. This means planning new programs and exhibits. The museum opened a temporary exhibit in 2014 that explores religion in Haiti. A temporary exhibit on Ancient Greece is also planned.

The Field Museum continues to plan new permanent exhibits like Evolving Planet to encourage people to visit the museum and learn about natural history.

Activity

The Field Museum pioneered the use of dioramas to show animals in their natural habitats. This allowed visitors to understand more about where these animals lived and what they ate.

Imagine that you are one of the Field Museum's curators and must design a diorama to display one of your favorite animals. Research that animal. Where does this animal live? Does your animal live alone or in a group? What other animals live in this area? What kind of plants grow in that environment? What does this animal eat?

Design Your Diorama

1. Find a plastic model or a picture of your animal.

2. Get a small cardboard box.

3. Use paint, felt pens, or colored pencils to draw the animal's habitat on the back of the box.

4. Continue the habitat at the front of the box by adding items such as rocks, moss, leaves, and twigs. Attach them to the box with glue, playdough, or putty.

5. Place your animal in its habitat.

6. Add other plants or animals that help your diorama tell the story of your chosen animal.

Field Museum Quiz

1 Where is the Field Museum located?

2 When did the museum open at its current site?

3 How much money did Marshall Field donate to the museum to help get it started?

4 What type of dinosaur was Sue?

5 Which exhibit shows 4 billion years of life on Earth?

ANSWERS:

1. Chicago, Illinois **2.** 1921 **3.** $1 million **4.** Tyrannosaurus Rex **5.** *Evolving Planet*

Key Words

biodiversity: the variety of life on Earth

collections: works of art or other items collected for exhibit and study in a museum, and kept as part of its holdings

conservation: the protection of something from deterioration

crystallizes: forms into crystals

curatorial: relating to the management, study, and care for a museum collection

deionized: removed charged atoms from a liquid

deoxyribonucleic acid (DNA): a molecule that contains genetic instructions that gives living things their characteristics

dioramas: three-dimensional models of a scene

ethnology: the study and comparison of different cultures and their characteristics

exhibit: a display of objects or artwork within a theme

expeditions: trips to collect objects or learn about something specific

fossils: remnants of animals or plants that lived long ago

fungus: an organism that feeds on organic matter

habitats: places where animals or plants usually live

humidity: moisture in the air

mercantile house: a place where business is conducted and goods are sold

naturalist: an expert in natural history

permanent exhibit: a display that a museum plans to keep in the museum for a long time

replica: exact copy

shrine: a place regarded as holy

three-dimensional: having an illusion of depth behind a flat surface

Index

Log on to www.av2books.com

AV² by Weigl brings you media enhanced books that support active learning. Go to www.av2books.com, and enter the special code found on page 2 of this book. You will gain access to enriched and enhanced content that supplements and complements this book. Content includes video, audio, weblinks, quizzes, a slide show, and activities.

AV² Online Navigation

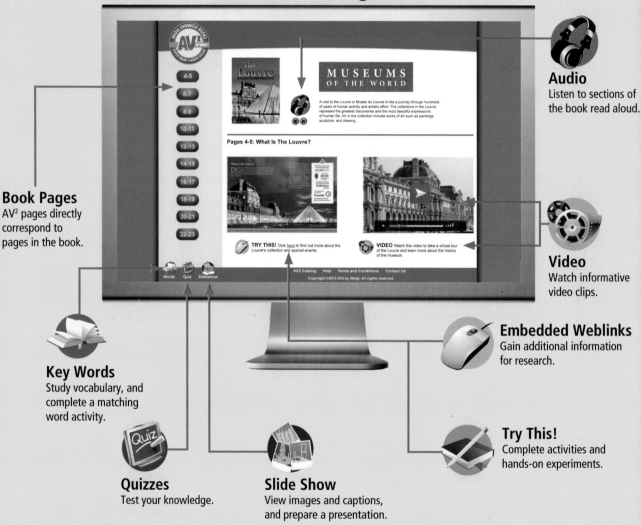

Book Pages
AV² pages directly correspond to pages in the book.

Audio
Listen to sections of the book read aloud.

Video
Watch informative video clips.

Key Words
Study vocabulary, and complete a matching word activity.

Embedded Weblinks
Gain additional information for research.

Try This!
Complete activities and hands-on experiments.

Quizzes
Test your knowledge.

Slide Show
View images and captions, and prepare a presentation.

AV² was built to bridge the gap between print and digital. We encourage you to tell us what you like and what you want to see in the future.

Sign up to be an AV² Ambassador at www.av2books.com/ambassador.